T0067162

The Girl in the Pink Beret

Who Sits Alone & Thinks in Silence

Written and Illustrated By:
Jackie Navielle

authorHOUSE®

AuthorHouse™ LLC
1663 Liberty Drive
Bloomington, IN 47403
www.authorhouse.com
Phone: 1-800-839-8640

Published by AuthorHouse   09/11/2014

ISBN: 978-1-4969-3936-4 (sc)
ISBN: 978-1-4969-3935-7 (e)

Contents

Part Four

Part Five

Part Six

Part One

Uncorrupt

Ch. 1

The Beginning

They were arguing. Something about what he forgot. Something about what she didn't do. I looked over at my sister, who five minutes ago, was sound asleep. She didn't look back at me though, her gaze stretched far beyond the window her eyes seemed glued to, and her stoic expression advised me to sit still and keep quiet. The arguing continued. Then the driver side door swung open; so hard that it swung back, nearly hitting my father as he franticly emerged from the car. With nothing in his hands and only the shirt on his back he began walking down the road in the direction we were already headed. My mother emerged from the car in a similar manner, only, she didn't follow my father down he unpaved stretch of old country road, on foot. She slammed the passenger side door closed, and hopped in the driver seat before starting up the car. My father didn't look as my mother drove slowly alongside him. His expression was coarse and manly, but looking at him closely, it looked as though he were about to cry. I had never seen my father cry. She cursed and screamed at him as she threw his belongings from the car. But still, he did not look our way. Focused on the road ahead of him his eyes grew red from straining to keep his composure and his fists swung like pendulums at his side. I watched my father closely, but silently, afraid their negativity would be turned at me if I tried to intervene. Enraged, my mother yanked off her wedding ring and threw it at him. It bounced off of him before landing in the dirt near his feet. My mother slammed her foot on the gas and made a U-turn creating a cloud of dust which engulfed my father. I turned completely around in my seat as tears began to fill my eyes. In the distance, I could see my father as he stooped down to pick up the ring. With tear filled eyes I looked over at my sister once more, only to see that her demeanor was unchanged, and so in unbeknownst, childish confusion, I sobbed inconsolably. The thought of losing my father hadn't even crossed my mind, but I cried duly, because my father was being left behind as we headed back home.

Four-o-clock in the morning; the ungodly time of day when most people are enjoying the last few hours, minutes and seconds of precious sleep they will need to overcome the day fast approaching. Although, my alarm-clock isn't set to go off until seven, a different high pitched annoyance has me awake, but not up. As I lie there, pretending to be asleep, my sisters baby demands attention. Her ear-splitting screams seem to awaken everyone but her mother. But still, I just lie there, after all, she's not my responsibility, I'm not the one who got knocked up last year. Finally, after what seemed like an endless bombardment of the world most harsh and foreboding sound, my sister emerged to put an end to the mini howling banshees' rage. That child was sent here to deafen the hearing and starve everyone out of house and home. A true plague sent from some fiery pit thousands of leagues under the earth's surface. Alas, these thoughts are draining, I have school in a few hours, *she* dropped out; leaving me all alone. High school is nothing but a breeding ground for everything adults fear. And for the most part, they have a right to fear it. Oh, the stories those walls could tell; if the buildings could talk, I bet they'd all need therapy. And yet, every day adults send us off to school, like soldiers off to war, and they're shocked when some of us don't make it home, or are changed, corrupted forever more. Society can be so cruel.

Ch. 2

Bad Brede

Reece and I met in kindergarten. She was new to the area and as the new kid she wanted to make new friends. However, she and I were not friends. As soon as she and I locked eyes, we were enemies. Reece constantly bragged about her father; who gave her whatever she wanted, even if the words, "I want," never crossed her lips. Lucky little Reece was an only child. A spoiled brat who had everything I didn't, including a lack of self-esteem and zero moral values. After months of constant bickering, teasing and a few minor fights, she moved away. I can't remember a more beautiful day; the clouds seemed to part just as her father's U-Haul disappeared into the distance. Birds chirped pleasantly from high atop the trees, Bee's buzzed gallantly riding the gentle breeze and I waved slowly with the warm feeling that came from not winning, but not losing either. But fate has a way of reconnecting people, with a few life lessons attached as an added bonus.

Reece and I met again in the sixth-grade. She was a *changed* individual. As a five-year-old, she had very long nearly straight hair, a pretty tan complexion and luminous hazel eyes that I childishly envied with every fiber in my being. But now, only five years and a few months later, I almost didn't recognize her, I almost began to pity her. Her thin, kinky, pinky length hair, her bruised and discolored skin spattered with freckles and zits and her eye's which were surrounded by dark circles had all but lost their luster. I felt bad, for not feeling bad for her, because she *was* pitiable, but even that was too much of an effort for a girl I used to hate with a broiling passion. The rumor was that her mother had passed away and her father got re-married. He happened to fall madly in love with a woman with a younger, prettier daughter, and with no need of an older one, poor Reece was cast aside. I can only imagine how she must have felt; losing her mother and her father's affection. It was a visible scar, one that changed her in more ways than I'm sure even she would admit to.

When it was time to go to high-school, she simply didn't care anymore. After discovering make-up and pushup bras, she had become a different type of "daddy's girl". Any man willing to pay, either with cash or attention, she was more than willing to call, "daddy". Countless rumors spread around school about her on a near daily basis, but she still kept a large, devoted following of brownnosers and sycophants. From atop her ego which she rode like a horse drawn carriage, she looked down her nose at me, tossing me a few insults here and there, just as she had so many years before. Unoffended by her two cent treats and half priced insults, I never paid her any attention. I figured Karma would handle her better than anything I could retaliate with, and I was right because when she got pregnant, no one wanted her or her baby. Her friends, her following, even her father kicked her to the curb, wanting nothing to do with "a needy whore," to quote her doting father. And like a magic trick, her social status went poof, and she too, disappeared from the high school scene. Unfortunately, I still have the misfortune of seeing her on a regular basis, but not as the rival I once fought; but as a sad excuse for a spoiled brat who lost it all.

Ch. 3

Tainted Flower

I met my best friend one summer in the girl scouts, her name was Nabara Rosanna. She didn't say much but she and I became instant friends. She told me that, Nabara, was not her first name but that I should call her by it, anyway. But staying true to my Americanism, I gave her a nick name instead, Nana. In the girl scouts, uniformity was key. All of us wore identical pink uniforms and a plethora of girlie accessories. What seven-year-old girl wouldn't want to? Being in the girl scouts is supposed to build character, help make friends and give young girls fun memories; a solid foundation to build a positive future around. But in every garden amongst the flowers there is a weed or two, a flower that is not like the rest, that's different and unwanted. Nana Rosanna was a dandelion amongst poppies. She had thin curly hair which all fit into one pudgy pigtail, was very tall and clumsy, and had a crippling speech impediment.

Putting all the negative things aside, she and I accepted one another as we were and formed a sisterly bond. Me and Nana told each other just about everything; what was cute to wear, what wasn't cute to wear, what foods were good and what foods to avoid, which boys were hot and which ones we despised. She only mentioned her brother a few times, never wanting to focus on him for very long. Although we spoke about a lot of things, nothing I could say would get Nana to show me her ever hidden wrists. And when I would ask her about her wrists she always changed the subject. Nana's wrists were always covered with bracelets, bangles and scrunchies, nothing unusual on a nice breezy day, but at the height of summer, it was a bit odd. Nana had told me once that she spent a lot of time by herself when she was at home because her brother was so mean to her and she wasn't allowed to go outside, but I never asked what she did in her alone time. Although Nana and I were inseparable, we were treated differently by the other scouts. While I was ignored completely, the girls in our troop teased Nana relentlessly, but she seemed to ignore it all. She was always so kind and forgiving, nothing they could do or say to her made her hate them. But little by little, the teasing seemed to be chipping away at her. She stopped wearing her pink uniform and started dressing in dark, depressing outfits. Troop leaders and a few of the older scouts tried reasoning with Nana, but eventually, the up-beat, overly happy atmosphere of the girl scouts was too much for my mild emotioned, dark cloud toting friend. So she dropped out.

Six years had passed before I saw Nana again, but not in person. Me and Nana lost contact after she left the girl scouts; which wasn't an unusual occurrence, but still quite a sad one. I would have preferred to see Nana, but for a time, I was happy just to see someone who was close to her. I only knew about Nana's older brother from her brief tongue slips and disdained rants of his ill will, even so, I didn't think he could be such a bad guy. Her older brother was a junior in high-school at the time he began happenstancly running into my big sister. I wonder if Nana knew her big brother had taken interest in my older sister. I wonder if Nana would have approved, or if she would have warned my sister of his evils. Nana once told me he called her a name in their native language, and after hearing what happened to her I Googled the translation; "lifeless whore," is what popped up as the top twelve results of the fourteen results listed, the last two came up as, "deceased whore," and "dead prostitute." I couldn't imagine why he'd call her such an awful name, unless something had actually happened to her. I figured that she might have been assaulted as a child. She must have seen no way to prove him wrong, so she decided to prove him right instead. She did something to show him, and everyone who had ever done her wrong, just how much of a lifeless whore she truly was. I wanted to warn my sister, but I was too overcome with grief to do much of anything. The only best friend I ever had killed herself. The news reporter said, "She slit one of her wrists and died in agonizing pain on the floor of her room." The picture they showed on the news was of her back from the girl-scout days, the good ol' days, dressed in her pink uniform and matching pink beret. But when they showed her lifeless corpse on the front page of the Sunday newspaper, the black and white page did her true disposition some justice.

Ch. 4

Stranger, Still

Jalisa, my older sister was a mouse, metaphorically speaking of course. But still, I clung to her like a boa constrictor to a mongoose. She was my role model and even though she was quiet and even a little standoffish at times, I learned more from her than I did from any teacher. She's three years older than me but she always treated me like we were equals, no matter how unfair it seemed at the time. She was always the strong one; the one who could take whatever the world through at her and it would never affect or change her. While I was always the one crying, she was always the one wiping away my tears. When our parents split, it was Jalisa who tried consoling me, who taught me to move on and to see the bright side of every situation. She was like a single candle in a dark room, luminous and warm. That is, until she went to high school. The idea of high school mesmerized me. I couldn't wait to go, but I began to lose my enthusiasm as Jalisa began to lose her mind.

Seeing a change in my sister, I confronted her. But to my dismay she wasn't bashful or embarrassed. The only thing that came to mind to ask her was, "what happened to you?" In a desperate attempt to find an answer, I looked deeply into her eyes searching for that one last piece of humanity hiding somewhere within the monster standing before of me. But instead of finding the answer I sought, I was left with more questions; that in my immaturity, I chose to leave unanswered. Jalisa had developed a new habit of laughing at me whenever I tried to talk to her one-on-one as we had in the past, and this time was no different.

I'll never forget her impulsive, boisterous response which consisted of one simple word, "Dick." Of all the ass-backwards things to say, the thing she blamed for her big change was, dick. "Ain't shit in this world better than some good dick," she told me ardently but warningly, before pushing me aside and walking away.

Within what seemed like a weeks' time, she was no longer the quiet, stoic and mildly aloof sister I loved and learned from. She was rude, disrespectful and uncaring. Jalisa chose boys over her family and sex over her morals. My once radiant candle had burned out leaving an empty pit of nothingness, nothing but a foul, lingering wisp of smoke that couldn't be caught or controlled. Jalisa started hanging out with Reece and Nana Rose's older brother, as if no other juvenile delinquents would do. At the advice of her new found friends, she got tattoo after tattoo until her body was a nothing more than a canvas with a few empty patches of skin left visible, many of which housed either a piercing or a gauged whole.

My dear sister became a whore, but I could still find it in my heart to love and forgive her because of the memories I continued to hold dear, but that changed when she decided to settle down. Of all the many men she slept with, she fell in love with the one, most detestable, distasteful, heathen this side of Hell. She knew I didn't like him, but she didn't care what I thought. I had one simple warning for her, but she chose to ignore my plea, "Irony is for the ill-fated." She and Nana Rose's brother had sex just once; a few days later her period never came and eight months after that she and Reece formed a common bond. I laughed when Jalisa told me she was pregnant, but when she told me the little bastard was conceived on my bed, I found nothing laughable. As far as I'm concerned, her and her little bastard can go somewhere far, far, far away and just leave me to my thoughts. I don't need her anymore; she served her purpose and continues to over stay her welcome, as most teenagers nowadays do.

Ch. 5

The Breadwinner

My mother has never won any mother of the year awards but she's still responsible for raising me, Jalisa and now, the little bastard, as well. To me, Lalaine has always been good old mommy dearest in the flesh. Over the years, to provide for the family my father chose to abandon, she's worked two full time jobs often taking extra shifts and making tips in anyway she could. Never having the energy or time for my sister and I, we basically raised ourselves. Therefore, we both got away with quite a bit, but not everything. Lalaine noticed when Jalisa got her first boyfriends name tattooed on her right arm, and her second boyfriends name tattooed on the left but my mother didn't seem to notice Jalisa's "condition" until she actually went into labor. And being the natural born nurturer she was she let her emotions consume her. Wanting only to stay home and take care of her "little bundle of joy", my mother went down to the bank the very next day after the birth of the bastard, returned with two fistfuls and a handbag full of cash, then in a single phone call, quit both of her jobs without a second thought. I watched my mother throw her life's hard work, and my possible college fund, away with tear filled eyes. Off the hook, Jalisa went back to her old ways and bad habits, Nana Rosanna's brother to be specific.

Despite my inane family, I went ahead and focused only on myself, taking on high school without any self-doubt or despair. High school really isn't so bad, as long as you're not trying to win any popularity contests. All you really have to do is go to class and count down the hours until you leave, without forgetting to avoid the bullies, insecure has-been's, jocks, jerks and perverse staff; Day by day, class by class, hour by demeaning hour, following the same grueling routine for roughly ten months out of the year.

Due to my lack of sleep thanks to the little banshee, today was especially tiring. Nowhere I went seemed to give me a break; a pop quiz in every class, detention during lunch and I missed my bus home after school. And with no cell phone to call home I was stranded, as if anyone would come get little-old-overlooked me, anyway. Finally after walking all the way home, I have the misfortune of seeing Reece sitting in the living room watching TV with the little bastard, as though she was an invited guest. She never seemed to bring her brat around so I assumed she dumped it in some infant care facility years ago. I asked her where my sister was but got no response, and then I heard some muffled chatter. I ignored it for a moment until I noticed its origin was none other than my room. With the might of the gods, I swung my room door wide open; promptly readying my meager list of slurs to throw at Jalisa and Nana's brother, but it wasn't Jalisa and her boy-toy thrashing in my sheets, it was a sight a million times worse. In a state of bewilderment I gasped, "Mom? Dad!?"

I averted my eyes and slammed the door shut. Then I took off down the hall way, but the throw-up escaped my mouth before I could reach the toilet. Jalisa walked by at that moment, stopping for a second to fully take in my misery then laughed before continuing on to the living room. As she joined Reece and the bastard on the couch she gallantly yelled, "hey Lil' Bit, dad's home." She and Reece laughed uncontrollably, but still throwing-up and sick from what I had just seen, I found nothing to laugh about, once more.

Ch. 6

Misplaced Love

After nine years of separation, they finally and unfortunately, reconnected. Lalaine was fresh out of high school when she and David first met. It was true love at first sight. Two months after their first kiss they were married and seven months after that they had my sister. And then came me, a surprising three years later. And five years after that, he forgot to delete the e-mails he received from his lover about their weekly excursions and she didn't use protection when she got her revenge, which in turn gave everyone involved in the little circle of sex, the Herp. David, feeling responsible for his young lovers unfortunate fate, went to be with her, rather than staying with his family. And although Jalisa and I had nothing to do with the whole debacle we suffered, too. After all, we never did make it to Disney Land. But the reason they reconnected all these many years later, was pure rotten luck, topped off a nice fat helping of bullshit.

David is and always was a man of habit, but things always seem to right themselves, though, nine times out of ten at someone else's expense. David went to the store to pick-up a winning lotto ticket, as he believed all his lotto purchases to be, only to find that his go-to Liquor store had been shut down due to a minivan lodged in the front counter. Remembering that the ghetto grocery store near his old home also sold "winning" lotto tickets, he went there instead. It just so happened, that Lalaine was also at that very same ghetto grocery store buying diapers for the bastard. Upon entering the store David and Lalaine spotted one another.

Mortified at the sight of his dearly beloved with a new baby, he ran to her ready to beat the father senseless and win her back in the process. Relieved at hearing the baby wasn't hers, but disappointed upon finding out who birthed Satin's spawn, he asked to come home to talk some sense into Jalisa. However, somewhere between making their way home and entering the house, my bed became their destination. After tiding themselves up and what I assume from the howling in the bathroom was a quickie, they announced they were renewing their vows and that David was coming home. I think they mistook my perturbed scream and the faint that followed as a sign of relief on my behalf, because several hours later when I came to, on the living room floor, it was apparent my condition was none of their concerns. Alone and left to my thoughts, I sat and brewed over my misfortune. I could have died and it wouldn't have even mattered. And what happened to David's precious, little, young whore?

Ch. 7

New Beginnings

After buying a new comforter and matching sheet set I finally feel comfortable sitting on my bed once more. I had been sleeping on the couch and might still; getting over traumatic situations take time after all. It's been almost two years since my father came home, a year since Jalisa moved in with Nana's Brother, leaving her baby here to torment me further, and in a few months I'll be gone. College, the final frontier as far as education goes, anyway. Somehow through the bickering and bullshit, tests and mountains of homework, rules and patronizing hours of class after class, I managed to escape the paper bound bonds of high school, uncorrupted. I don't really know what to expect from college but as long as it's nothing like high school I'll be alright. And now that the bastard has learned to walk, her screams and rants have become mobile, and that's all the more reason to leave.

Sometimes I wonder if Nana was still here, would she and I even still be friends, if we'd go to the same college like we'd planned or if we'd be distant friendly figures from days long passed, as she is to me now. I almost hate that I knew her. When someone dies, is murdered or commits suicide, it's one thing, but knowing that person, sharing memories with that person; she was my best friend. I could have tried to help her, I wasn't blind, I saw the signs but chose to ignore them all, to sit and judge. It's the same with Jalisa and Reece. If I was there for her when her mom died, maybe Reece and I could have found a way to reconcile our differences. Hell, then maybe I'd have a friend now. And as much as I hate Jalisa now, I do wonder if it's my fault for her being the way she is. Sure I didn't force a dick in her face, or anywhere else, but in a way, I forced her to seek comfort elsewhere; I drained her mentally with all my whining and crying, never giving her a listening ear or shoulder to cry on. Maybe, if I wasn't so clingy she wouldn't resent me so. I couldn't help my parents, don't think I would have known how, honestly. And to be frank I still can't look either of them in the face without their expressions and moans from the *incident*, popping into my head clear as day. I am a troubled soul, as we all are, in a way.

These tiresome thoughts are disheartening, but maybe, I have been the corrupt one all along. I haven't been uncorrupted by the world as I've believed for all these many years. Maybe I've been the one corrupting others, by not fixing the flaws I saw and let fester. If only I could rewind time and make that added effort. But alas, the world spins in a single direction and time runs its course uninhibited, unempathetically. And just as the world is the world, with little variations and a lot of room for improvement, I am who I am and jaded as I may be, in my mind I will always remain, uncorrupt.

Part Two

Bad Ambition

Ch. 1

First Betrayal

"Don't go," I whined as she slung her duffle bag over her shoulder. "Please, don't leave me."

She looked at me with a smile and said, "baby sis, you've gotta walk on your own two feet and live by your own accomplishments." As she picked up her bag and sat in the open window she gave me one last bit of advice, "you can't rely on anyone to give you what you want, you have to take charge and do thing to benefit yourself. No one will just hand you everything you need in this life, especially not men. Don't trust any man, ok. Baby sis, promise me you won't ever rely on men."

I looked down and through the tears I mumbled, "I promise," and when I lifted my head my big sister was gone. Marie was eleven years older than me but from a maturity stand point she was already an adult. When she ran away from home I wanted to hold on to her words. I wanted to believe that her advice was some sort of beacon. As though somehow, by following her advice there was a way for her to come find me again one day. But things change. Life has a way of distorting memories, stretching truths and even hope, given time, fades to despair and disillusionment. I once saw every bit of my older sister in myself, because I loved her and wanted nothing more than to be just like her. But I came to realize that I wasn't anything like her, we didn't even look alike, all we shared was a few memories of us laughing together and the secret of the night she left. Rather than hold on to the hope of seeing my dearly beloved sister again, I began wishing for her never to return. I hated her last words, which played over and over in my mind; she didn't even say goodbye, or wish me well. I wanted a better sister, so I sought friendship, because sometimes blood isn't as binding as we think. And after a while Marie was never mentioned or spoken of, she simply didn't exist anymore, and in a way, I was glad.

Ch. 2

Finding Loss

When I caught my dad having an affair with the school nurse we moved to a new house, a new neighborhood and I was enrolled in a new school. To help me settle in, my mom took me on a tour of the neighborhood in our car. But as I looked out the window nothing really fazed me, it was all the same, the houses all looked alike, the cars, the dogs, the people walking, but then something caught my eye. There were two girls playing together, they looked like sisters. Then I realized that's how me and Marie should have been; we never played together. As we passed, time seemed to be moving at a snail's pace, and with each lingering second that I stared at the two entranced in play, I grew envious, jealous and bitter.

Dad bought me all sorts of things and even if I didn't say anything about wanting it, he still bought it, all he'd ever say was, "Old memories don't beat new toys." Basically meaning he wanted me to forget everything bad that had happened since my sister left, including his affair, and to help my memories fade I was showered with countless toys and sweets, vacations and shopping sprees. I adored my father, even though he'd hurt my mom and made her cry, I still loved him more than anyone. After my sister left he was the main one, who was always there for me, and I wanted that feeling to last forever, and in my youth, I believed it would.

"What's your name?" my new classmates swarmed me and spread news of my arrival throughout the entire elementary school, I was the one they all buzzed about but that wasn't good enough. I knew that I could easily be the queen. Amidst the crowded classroom, I saw the girl I had seen playing with her sister and glared at her. She didn't seem to mind and that was enough to send me over the edge, I vowed to myself then, to take the one thing she had that I didn't, her sister. But before I chose to extend my hand in sisterhood to a girl I didn't even know, I expanded and enforced my rule over my classmates. Only, my reign was short lived.

Just as soon as we'd moved into the new house in the new neighborhood, my dad had been acquaintancing himself with some new pussy. My mom's only response to this reoccurring problem was the same as before, she chose to leave and move us all, elsewhere. But fate intervened. With dad and I in the U-Haul and mom trailing us in the car we made our way down the long stretch of freeway as rain began to fall. Before long we were sitting in traffic in the midst of a downpour. I huffed on the window and doodled with my index finger. Dad was on the phone with some woman and in the back of my mind I wondered what she was like. A few police cars zoomed by on the other side of the road followed by an ambulance but I didn't really care to ask dad where they were going. He was still laughing and baby talking his lover. After a while of stop and go traffic, the flow of all the cars began to pick up speed and the rain began to lighten. I looked in the rear view mirror to see if my mom was still behind us only to realize that she was not.

"Where'd mom go." I demanded to know forcing my father to look in his side view mirror.

"Hang on hun," he pulled over to the side of the highway then apologized to his lover before hanging up and dialing my mom. He called her several times but got no answer. An ambulance sped by, this time on our side of the highway. My dad suggested that we continue on ahead and meet up with her later, so he left her a voice mail and we continued onward.

"I'm hungry." My stomach had been growling for some time but I figured now was the best time to get something to eat without my mom interfering and saying how unhealthy fast food was.

"Alright princess, how about we go get you a burger?" My face lit up, but as we made our way to the off-ramp, my dad's phone rang. He answered it, being more standoffish and gruff at first, but then he began to tremble and plead with whomever it was he was talking with. Rather than go get burgers my father got back on the freeway in the same direction we were already headed and drove like a mad man until we reached a hospital. "Stay here." He instructed, as he got out of the truck and hurriedly rushed to the emergency entrance. I got out of the truck and followed him instead, but he didn't seem notice. After turning a few corners and heading down a corridor or two, I was hopelessly lost. After roving for a bit I found myself wandering the long halls and happened to see a girl walking down one of the halls. "Marie!" she seemed preoccupied and didn't hear me so I ran to her, but just as I did, she went down another hall, then another, and another. I followed her relentlessly, but every time I thought I had caught up to her, she was even farther away. She turned a corner and disappeared once more but I was determined to find her so I zoomed past a waiting area and found myself in front of an elevator. The doors had closed only seconds before my arrival so I figured patience would be the key to finding my sister.

Ch. 3

Dethroned

As I stood in front of the elevator door, awaiting my sister's return, a security guard took me away. At first I sheepishly flowed but as we got farther from the elevator I began to yell and scream. It wasn't my father I was searching for anymore, it was my sister but the security guard didn't seem to care. I continued to cry and scream as he took me by the hand and led me to my dad. When I saw my dad sitting in a chair next to a room, I ran to him.

"Dad, dad guess who's here..." my dad seemed to ignore me and as I got a better look at his face I asked, "are you ok? Dad?" His eyes were red, his nose was running and he was pale in the face. He patted his lap and told me to sit down.

I sat on his lap and he hugged me, while holding me tightly he whispered in my ear, "Rena is dead... your mom... she's... dead." I shook myself free of his grip and ran into the room only to see that there was no one in it. Both beds were empty and freshly made. I ran out the room and started to run down the hall back in the direction of the elevators but my dad swooped me up and held me as I cried. After crying myself to sleep I awoke alone in the chair, where my dad had been sitting. I got up and peaked into the room I had run into before and saw my father holding and kissing a woman, passionately. In a half sleep, I ran to her, thinking it was my mom. But as I got closer I realized that she was definitely no mother of mine.

"Hi here..." She said to me smiling, as she looked to my father for reassurance, "Reece, hey... um... sorry about your... uh." She nudged my dad and took a step back.

"Princess, this is daddy's friend, Ms. Laila. Ms. Laila also has a little girl and-" she cut him off whispering something about him calling me, princess. Apparently that was her little brat's nickname as well and she wanted it to be hers exclusively. "Any way, we're going to go stay with Ms. Laila and her daughter for a while, okay?" He didn't wait for my approval before he began smiling and giggling with this whore and that's when I realized just how much I meant to him. If he could get over my mother so fast then what about me? Clearly I too, meant nothing to him or Marie. It was a truly a dark day, because on that day, I lost everything.

"Who's she supposed to be."

"Milaina, be nice, this is your new big sister, Reece." Laila was doing her best to have her brat except the fact that from now until they found a new place to live, we'd be sharing a room. Milaina was two years younger than me but had me matched when it came to complaining and getting whatever she wanted.

"Daddy," I whined, "why can't I have my own room?"

"Because, sweetie, there simply aren't enough rooms for you to have your own." Dad was doing his best to get me to cooperate, but neither me nor the brat were willing to give in. Unfortunately for me though, this meant that I went without a bedroom altogether, and for the first time, I slept on a couch in a stranger's home.

Ch. 4

Second Betrayal

Not knowing how exactly to do my hair, Laila, chose not to do it at all. Instead of combing it, I would just run my fingers through it, which eventually caused my long nearly straight hair to break, dread and split at the ends. And with no room to call my own, I remained in the living room; meaning that when my father got home from work at one in the morning and when Laila left out to go to work at five, I was awoken and my face showed just how tired I always was. At school I was teased and fell behind in my schoolwork which didn't bother me much but I hated how much my dad complained about it; so I began bullying a nerd or two into doing my homework, but after seeing how easily Laila got my father to pay her bills and do things for her, I found a new way to get things done. Rather than be a bully, I started flirting to get my way, and it worked like a charm but I knew I would have to up my game if I wanted things like Laila. Although I hated her with every fiber of my being, I found it more beneficial to be like her than anyone else I'd ever seen or met. She was my role model.

When it was time to head to middle school, my dad and Laila announced to Milaina and I that we'd be moving back to the old house in the suburbs. The very same house my mother died trying to leave. I objected of course but nothing I said or did mattered.

"Don't you want your own room?" Dad asked me, but all the while looking at Laila.

"Sure, that'd be great but there's only two bedrooms in the old house, Dad." I said graciously but with a hint of annoyance in my tone.

"Well," he said throwing his hand in the air, "guess you and Milaina will have to share the master bedroom and Laila and I will have to stay in your old room. How's that sound?" Milaina began crying, open mouthed and loudly like a toddler who'd just dropped their ice cream. "It's ok, Milaina, we'll figure it out."

"It's all about poor little Milaina, no one cares about what I want!" I exclaimed, only to be slapped across the face. My face swole-up and my light complexion made the bruise look more like I'd been beaten repeatedly. My father hit me the way he used to hit my mother, only I did not cry like she did, I would not be silenced so easily. "I hate you." I said it just loud enough for him to hear, but low enough for it not to offend him.

It was less than a week later, when we moved and I was once again new to the area. Although my appearance had changed quite a bit, deep down I was the same as I'd always been, ruthlessly ambitious. I knew that with a little effort and the right amount of followers, I could once again be queen. But unlike when I was in kindergarten, I was talked about behind my back, all those friends I had made were nowhere to be found and only my enemy remained. I had to start at the bottom and work my way up the social ladder, but I was fine with that, because I knew how to get what I wanted, Laila was my blueprint.

Ch. 5

Re-Birth

By the time high school rolled around I was ready to ascend to my thrown. With the power of make-up, push-up bras, and a couple lace thongs, I was the envy of every girl and the fantasy of every guy. After losing my virginity, sex was no longer something I valued, it was just something I did to pass time and to get out of the house, mainly, to get out of the living room which my dad dared to call *my* room. I was content being called a slut, by everyone including my dad, so long as I had my looks, my followers and my petite figure, I was just fine. Not to mention all the girts, treat, perks and money I received non-stop. And for a while I was ok with just being handed things, but I knew my time in high school would be short lived and I needed something that would last long after classes ended.

My goals had not changed from elementary school, and I still hated that little tacky girl, whose sister I had declared to claim but I had to put that plot on the backburner. Jealously is a plague and wantonness is a virus, both spread throughout my high school at a dizzying pace. Rumors spread throughout my school like a wildfire but I denied them all, and my dedicated group of flunky's assured me that none of the rumors held any ground. But deep down the pressure was eating me alive. I became queen but maintaining my throne was becoming more strenuous and tiresome than I'd imaged. My life was being fast-forwarded and I was having trouble keeping up. I focused less on academia and more on appearances. I cared more about the latest gossip than the credits I was lacking. I was more concerned with making other girls hate me than bothering to make and maintaining friends. I began losing control over myself and started doing things I regretted more and more, until finally, I went too far.

I took my first ever pregnancy test in the last stall of the girls restroom on the first floor of my high school during the only time of day it'd actually be empty, lunch. It wasn't that I cared if people knew whether I was pregnant or not, I just didn't know what my reaction would be, and that was something I couldn't have everyone knowing. The empty silence was only broken by the eerie dripping of one of the many faucets. When I looked down and saw the results, I didn't cry, or sigh, or even smirk, I just looked at it. The two double lines confirmed what I already knew to be true. I was pregnant and by whom... *well*. As much as I tried to hide my condition, residing in the living room made hiding anything difficult and before long Laila began to have her suspicions. After seeing me throw up just before she left for work one morning, she confronted me.

"How much of whore do you have to be to get knocked up at seventeen?" she laughed as she twirled her drink, which of course was a concoction of none other than, a few cubes of ice, grape juice, apple juice, V8 juice and Crown Royal; such a *wonderful* role model. While she looked down her nose at me she took a sip before saying, "just you wait 'til your father hears this juicy bit of scandal." I glared at her, but the vomit prohibited me from responding, even though I had some good comebacks just waiting to come out once my throwing up was finished. "I think I'll wait to tell him over lunch. You know Tuesdays are our lunch date days, after all." She emphasized each word trying to strike fear in my heart, but all I felt was sick, and nothing she said could make me feel worse or anything otherwise.

By the time school ended for the day I had forgotten Laila's words. With it being finals, school let out early but with nothing better to do I stayed at the school, hanging out with the circle of sycophants I referred to loosely as 'friends.' When my father's car pulled up I didn't think much of it, but when he got out of the car and marched over to me with fire in his eyes and steam bellowing from his ears, my first thought was, 'run!'

"You!" was the first word he said to me while shaking his finger in my face. The words that followed weren't so friendly, or pleasant. "You can go do whatever you like… whomever you like, I don't care anymore. I don't need you, your sister, or your mother! And I definitely don't need some bastard kid running around *my* house, it's bad enough that you're there taking up my living room space." he paused to wipe the sweat from his upper lip before continuing a bit more quiet and intently. My enemy was walking past just as he spoke, I tried my best to keep my composure but rage made my fists shake and I closed my eyes and tilted my head down in defeat. "I have no room in my life or my house, for a needy whore. You got that?" I just stared at him in disbelief as he tossed a few dollars at my feet and walked away. Milaina was in the back seat of the car laughing hysterically and Laila was in the front seat smirking at me. I gave them all the middle finger but as I looked around for my 'friends' to console me and tell me how everything was going to be ok, all I were their backs. I was once again alone.

Ch. 6

Final Betrayal

I wandered the streets for a while until it got dark, with only twenty seven dollars left from the thirty my dad had given me I didn't have enough to get a hotel room or even enough to call a cab back to the house. So I just sat down at a bus stop and waited. Every few minutes or so a pervert would pull over and ask me if I needed a ride, I declined of course but got tired of constantly having to explain to them that I was perfectly fine. After the moon had risen completely and hardly anyone was walking around, another car pulled up but this time a familiar voice called out to me.

"Baby sis!" Marie and I stared at each other with open mouths, her eyes began to fill up with tears and against my will, my eyes did the same. I got in her car and we sat and hugged for a few minutes saying how much we missed each other before she was able to wipe away her tears and drive. "Why are you out so late? Want me to take you home?"

"Dad kicked me out." I said it casually but I nearly began to cry after the words left my lips. "because I'm pregnant."

"Aww, don't cry, it'll be OK." She tried consoling me but nothing worked then she added, "well what did mom say? I'm sure she won't just let him do that."

I put my head down, not exactly sure how to tell her about our mom, so I just said it flat out, "she died... years ago." Marie hit the brakes and the car came to a screeching halt. She didn't say anything or even look at me, she just whipped away the tear and continued driving.

In a very low tone she asked, "how'd it happen?"

I told her everything that happened since she left which led to me telling her about Laila and Milaina, me not having a room, my time in school and even about my pregnancy and before either of us even realized it the sun was coming up and we were in her room with an empty box of pizza and a flat diet cola. We hadn't even noticed that her longtime boyfriend had returned from his long night of 'hanging out with the boys.'

After regaling her of my life without her, Marie told me to stay and live with her. She cleared out her home-office, bought furniture online and before I could even object, she wrote my name on the door in orange lipstick and ushered me into my new room. After a while of hanging out with her, I began going to the movies and to the mall alone. Some say patience is a virtue, but being the spoiled brat I was deep down I hated having to wait for things I wanted, but one thing that I had wanted since childhood came to me after over ten years of waiting.

"Must be boring, being here alone."

"I guess," I looked back to see who was talking to me but I didn't recognize her.

"Hi," she extended her hand to me. "I'm...uhh... Jalisa."

I shook her hand not knowing whether or not Jalisa was in fact her name but after hanging out together that day at the mall we became friends. It was only after going to her house that I realized who she was; my new friend Jalisa, was my kindergarten rivals older sister, the very same sister, I vowed to one day possess. This made our friendship all the more valuable and rewarding.

After the birth of my son, it was Marie who took care of him night and day. I was irritated by the name she gave him, but couldn't find a reason to really stop her from calling him by it. 'Nick-names are ok,' I thought. I didn't want to be a mother and it showed, I began leaving him with her for days on end while I hung out with Jalisa and Kevin, an unlikely friend of hers. None of us seemed to have anything in common but it was clear that all he wanted was sex and he'd put up with anything me and Jalisa did to get it. It was only a matter of time before Jalisa wound up pregnant and like me, she didn't have any interest in being a mom. But sometimes I wonder, maybe I sought the wrong friend.

Ch. 7

Undeterred

After years of hanging out and many fun times had, David left Marie and she fell into a deep depression. Right after that I stopped hanging around Jalisa. It wasn't that I didn't want to hang out with her and Kevin, anymore; it was just too awkward knowing that her dad and my big sister had been together for some years. It was almost sad the way it happened to. Marie seemed to be so in love, and now she seemed lost without him. As though a piece of her very being had been gutted and incinerated. For a time I felt that leaving my baby with her was helping her, but it later became obvious that she was dangerous. I began spending more time with my son after he called me auntie. I wasn't alarmed, because in truth I wasn't really around like a mother should have been, but the fact that my sister had tricked my son into believing she was his mother scared me for some reason. One afternoon after an argument I decided not to return to my sister's home. That small apartment wasn't big enough for the both of us, especially with my son there. So with the few dollars in my pocket and the money I had been letting grow in my savings account, I rented an apartment of my own.

So now, with only my son and no one else beside me, no education to stand on and only ambition as my guide, I have some new goals and aspirations. With Laila as my living example, I intend to attain the world.

Part Three

Ill-fated Irony

Ch. 1

On The Surface

I never thought I'd be the type of person to trade sunshine for shadows, gold for silver and life for, well, you get the point. I was once a very enthusiastic, fun-loving girl, but things changed. Or, maybe I'm wrong. Maybe the only thing that's changed is me. It must have started when I was little, when I realized that things weren't as they appeared. My mom wasn't happy, my father wasn't happy, my brother wasn't happy, even the dog wasn't happy. Yet, I forced myself to emit happiness and blissful obliviousness, because that's what little girls are supposed to do. I was a good little girl. I did everything I was supposed to do, but most of the time, it seemed that all my efforts were in vain. I wanted to exceed expectations and go above and beyond what limitations I faced. Even as a small child, I wanted to hold the world in my hands and be praised and respected, loved and adored. Life has a way of setting people in their place, but in my case, it's as though I'm just life's punching bag. Everything I ever did backfired, and with consequences that far exceeded the cause and left me with less than I started with, in most cases.

Ch. 2

Life Lessons

Once when I was very little, I wanted to be pretty. I say it was a 'onetime thing' because it kind of was. I was just beginning to understand what was pretty and what was ugly; what was wanted and what was discarded. I knew my mother was pretty, smart and adored by those around her. And although I was too, I wasn't respected like she was. I couldn't make demands, or even ask for much of anything that didn't need a 'please,' attached. I figured it must have had something to do with her appearance. So I tried putting on her heels to be talker. But the only thing I achieved by doing so, was falling and twisting my ankle. Then I tried putting on her clothing, but nothing fit me and I ended up tripping and falling once more. So, to forgo any chance of tripping and falling again, I decided to look like her on a smaller scale. I took her favorite lipstick and painted myself from head to toe with the soft, butter-like lipstick, not forgetting my fingertips, either. While I was just about to finish, my mom found me sitting on the bathroom floor covered in red, and screamed in disbelief. Needless to say, it was not the reaction I was expecting. I cried of course, and made myself promise never again to put on any make-up. I guess I kind of have a fear of the stuff now, but that's ok with me, because I'm not a very shallow person.

Ch. 3

Days of Ignorance

When I got my first pet, it seemed too good to be true; maybe because it was. It was a hamster, which I named and renamed every few hours and fed on a somewhat consistent hourly basis. I never knew if it was a boy or a girl, but it seemed like a boy, if that even makes any sense. I like to think that by spending time with animals, their personalities become more prevalent and they become more of a friend, than a caged beast. I may as well go ahead and say it; I killed that poor little thing. Not on purpose by any means, it was purely accidental. Actually, when I did it, I didn't even realize what I'd done. Being a kid, I knew what hurt and what didn't, to an extent. Falling from the couch or a chair to the floor below wasn't very pain inflicting at all. I had fallen on the carpet a few times, sometime repeatedly and didn't think anything of it, but when my poor hamster fell and didn't get up, I modestly thought he was just tired. So I put him back in his cage, covered him over with wood-shavings and went about my business. After watching cartoons for a few hours, I remembered my slumbering pet, and went to fetch him. But after feeling how cold and stiff he was, I knew he was dead. So I did what any guilty child does, I played dumb with a capital 'D.' I think that was my last hamster, too.

Ch. 4

Stunted

As I grew taller I expected to fill out in other places, but sadly I did not. While my fellow classmates were growing exponentially, I was still wearing clothing I'd gotten as a toddle. Even now, I wear pajamas from when I was three and four years old. I know I've grown taller, but nothing else seems to be catching up. One of my classmates even had the nerve to call me a hermaphrodite. After an intent dictionary search and a bit of asking around, I found out what it meant and rather than denounce the statement completely, I began to really wonder if I was. So I asked my parents, and of course, begin parents, they assumed this meant I needed, 'the talk.' For that one occasion, having an older brother, was worth all the harassment and torment. Because he had not yet gotten 'the talk,' our parents decided to hold off on telling me anything. They did, however, tell me that I was not a hermaphrodite, and that I'm just a late bloomer. So for a few months or so after that, I thought I was some type of hybrid flower.

Ch. 5

The Truth of Friendship

Every summer from the time I was five, I was sent off during the day to camps and clubs. I was always hesitant about going, but always had fun and made wonderful memories. One summer, I went to the Girl Scouts and met, perhaps, the strangest girl to ever exist. She was nosy, and boisterous and even a bit neurotic, but she said we were best friends. The only thing I really understood about friendship at the time was what I learned from TV. So I tried making as many friends as possible, but that seemed to push people away even more. The only person who didn't seem to mind my awkward want to make friends was that strange girl. I really can't even say that I remember anything about her beyond that, I sort of remember what she looked like, but I don't think I ever knew her name. Some people are just so easily forgettable.

Around that time though, I stated seeing things for what they really were. I like to think it was the cause of some great epiphany I had, but the real cause is not so grand. I was teased constantly; I was pushed and shoved, stepped on and ignored. Although, many times I wanted to lie down and cry my eyes out, I tried my best to ignore the never ending torment. I was used to the teasing and hazing to a certain degree, having an older brother meant I knew what a fight and an argument were. Kevin was not the loving older brother our parents thought him to be, and I was not the adoring little sister, I sanguinely portrayed. I am a pacifist, always have been one, and I like being one. But as a girl transitioning from playing with Barbie's to my tomboy phase, I wished to be a tyrant, a powerful person who everyone feared and respected. No one, not even my dog seemed to respect me; and not much has changed since then.

Bright things made me anxious and fun made me long for solitude. When I overheard my parents talking about getting a divorce, I gave up on trying to do my best. I gave up being happy, and fun-loving. I began to hate things I once loved. Anything cutesy, was no longer appealing to me. But when I was kicked out of the girl scouts for defying dress code, I regretted my change. I even tried to go back to the way I was, but this only confused me. I began questioning who I was and what I wanted in life. Questions I have yet to find the answer to.

Ch. 6

By Example

Depression is not one of those things which requires an age limit. Neither are thoughts of suicide. I was one push away from going over the edge. I was one step away from oblivion. I was helpless, lost, and friendless, I was... afraid.

Too cowardice to take my own life, I chose to let fate decide my future. I lived recklessly doing whatever seemed dangerous or life-threatening. I took handfuls of pain medication for the smallest aches and pains, I jaywalked whenever I felt like it, I left knives and scissors laying around chaotically, I even taunted random dogs I encountered. When Kevin saw how I was acting and the things I was doing, he began distancing himself from me even more. He stopped teasing and tormenting me, he stopped the hazing and harassment, he chose to focus his attention on another. I hated him for it, not because I wanted him all to myself, but because he was making my reckless thought process all the more easy. After the divorce papers were finalized, my mother left my father. And although she promised Kevin and I that once she found a good job and nice home she'd send for us, that day never came. Father said she took her life, but Kevin didn't believe him. He accused him of being a liar and a murderer, but I knew that mother was capable of suicide. Not because she was always sad or depressed, but because she was also happy and overly enthusiastic; it had to be draining.

Ch. 7

A Chance Encounter

Sometimes the things we think we want but do not receive or attain are simply put on hold. One breezy day, I was about to walk crassly into the street, when someone grabbed me from behind halting my advance just as a bus zoomed past. I turned around to see who'd grabbed me; ready to curse them out, but instead I was caught in a state of bewilderment. Standing before me was a woman, who seemed to be very distraught. Her eyes were red, her make-up was smeared all over her face and her nose was running. She asked me I was ok, I nodded wanting to ask her if she was ok. We ended up talking for a few minutes before we parted ways. She gave me a bit of advice then turned around and disappeared into the crowd. Of all the people on that busy street, the one who chose to save me was the one who probably needed saving too. I thought about the woman's selflessness, and realized how much I had to be grateful for. But sometimes, that little push into the light isn't enough to melt away the years of isolation and bad habits.

Ch. 8

Wise Words

I won't say that I did it on purpose but I don't think it was much of an accident either. I think it must have been fate. I remembered the words I had been told by that strange girl I met that summer in the girl scouts, "Irony is for the ill-fated." It was just one of those days when I wasn't feeling to well. I had a headache, stomach ache and was overly exhausted for no apparent reason. I sipped cold medicine straight from the bottle, I took a handful of pills then I realized something was wrong. My body was heavy and the most basic of movements took immense concentration. I was too out of it to even gather words to cry out for help. My cell phone sat perched casually on the edge of my desk which was only a few steps from my bed. I tried to get out of bed to get it, but ended up stumbling before falling to the floor instead. My cell phone fell, and bounced on the hardwood floor, landing several feet away. I looked over at it desperately trying to gather myself to be able to reach it but I could feel a strange sensation coming from my left arm. Out of sheer reflex, in an attempt to brace myself before hitting the cold, solid floor, I had put my hands out in front of me as I fell. Half tangled in my blanket, I laid on the floor bleeding; apparently I had fallen on a pair of scissors, which were now protruding from my left wrist. At that moment I remembered the distraught woman's advice, "watch your step, carelessness is the expressway to deaths door."

Part Four

Detached

Ch. 1

Preexistence

I'm sure it was crying. It didn't have to do it but it did, willingly, selflessly. I wasn't going to make it. I could feel myself fading back into the very mass that had created me. It didn't want to be alone, but it did not intend to sacrifice it's whole self in the process. Because of my cowardice, my thoughtless, uncaring, self-centered action, it lost more than it had bargained for. We were originally one, a single body and mind, split in two, but I was weak; too weak to survive on my own, and so it clung to me and we became one once more. But not a single consciousness, as before, even now, it still lingers in the depths of my mind. Bound in thought and locked away, and ever present. My other self, my look alike, my twin.

Ch. 2

Who I was

"No one likes a cry baby," my mom said that a lot, but in a joking, loving tone that always made me smile and wipe away the tears. I wasn't very outspoken and stayed to myself. I was now five and the memories I was burdened with in my earlier years faded to nothingness. The other 'me' was silent; there, but not there, just watching and waiting. Perhaps if I had acknowledged that other part of myself all along, or if that other self, had called out to me sooner, maybe the outcome could have been different and I'd still be the me I was. In my youth, I was the short, shy, quiet girl who didn't say much to anyone and played alone. I wasn't very pretty or talented and worried more about my classwork than stealing candy or what the newest, coolest dolls were. Basically, I was a target.

Elementary school is a jail, and in that jail, there is a hierarchy. At the top is the principal, then their close staff, then teachers, then the teacher's assistants, then the lead kiss asses, followed by the cool kids and their followers, the smart but cool kids, the geeks, the nerds, then the cry baby's, and lastly the weird kids. And I suppose I drew the short end of the stick. Because it didn't take much to make me cry and because I stayed to myself I was also labeled the "weird kid" too. As if it wasn't bad enough that I was weird and unwanted by my classmates at school, at home my baby sister seemed to despise me all the more. But I embraced my individualism and still did my best to be a good role-model for my much younger look alike, to an extent.

I hated the thought of her being treated the way I was, so I often pushed her away and always told her not to be like me. I even stopped calling her by her name and gave her a pet name, 'Lil' Bit.' I'm sure this confused her, but it was necessary. It was one thing to be teased and mistreated by others, but I began having depraved thoughts and hearing a voice in my head which beckoned for evil deeds to be committed by my hands. When I once shared one of my malicious plots with her, she seemed enthusiastic to help me in any way she could. Of course I was worried by this, and felt she was far too impressionable to be around and possibly corrupt.

In the back of my mind, I knew the bad thoughts were not my own, but I still could not bear to impose them on someone I loved so dearly, someone so young and oblivious to all the evils of the world. I can still remember crying after my classmates would tease me. They teased me about all sorts of stupid things. They said I was too dark to be pretty but to light to be one of them. They said my big lips were like those of a fish and that I walked with my butt poked out, even though I did no such thing. But I took all those things to heart. I was so very easily influenced back then. I wanted to fit in but the voice in my head told me not to, it sought rebellion and revenge. During the time, I generally refer to as childhood, I still had full control over myself, but even then I could feel my mental hold over myself slipping from my feeble grasp.

I began to pay more attention to the voice in my head around the time my dad began taking me on day trips to visit my aunt, Marie. Whenever I'd see her, the voice would frantically say, "that's not our aunt! And you know it. But you're too afraid to tell mom because you think you'll get daddy in trouble." The voice was right.

Ch. 3

My Second Self

For my eighth birthday my mom and dad planned a surprise trip to Disney Land but forgot that I could read lips and the brochure they left laid out around the house unknowingly. I was so elated about the trip that I even told Lil' Bit, but made her promise not to tell anyone else. I remember how happy I was. I was ok with the super long drive there and back; all that mattered was getting there and having fun. But along the way everything went terribly wrong.

They were arguing. Aunt Marie had called dads phone and mom answered it; and after a brief chat and what seemed like a pleasant 'good bye,' my mom got angry. Very, very angry. She started going through his phone, then she started screaming, "there's the proof right there!" Dad didn't break his gaze on the road ahead when he mumbled something under his breath; mom stopped screaming, but the argument continued in a more intent and quieted fashion. I hated when they argued but I was comforted by the fact that my little sister was a heavy sleeper. At least she didn't have to be witness to this farce. The voice in my head was chanting, "all-your-fault! All-your-fault!" The arguing continued growing louder by the word until they were both screaming at one another.

After a while I fell asleep and even in my dreams I was denied the solace of peace and tranquility. The other part of me that seemed to have taken up residence in my thoughts had a new name for itself. It whispered to me in my dreams, telling me to call it and refer to it as, "Other Self." Because, little did I know, Other Self, was becoming a permanent part of me. While my parents continued their argument, by this time having already pulled over to the side of the road, I tried to find peace by looking out the window, down the narrow column of trees that seemed to extend in an infinite number of rows for a million miles. As I tried to count the rows I could feel my mind being overrun with, Other Self's thought's. It was as though my mind was about to explode. I felt completely hopeless and chose to ignore the pitiful, confused look on my little sister's tiny face. When my dad finally emerged from the car and began walking down the dirt road, I knew that was it. I was losing my mind and my parents.

Ch. 4

The Me, I Became

By the time middle school rolled around Other Self was beginning to take control of my body, gave me advice from time to time, and even started speaking out on our behalf. At times, when I was overwhelmed by my shyness or spinelessness, I'd let Other Self take over. Other Self was the *me* that was unafraid of consequences, leaving me to be the one reprimanded. I never told anyone about that darker side of me. As I began blooming into a young woman Other Self was the part of me that would flirt with guys, but after losing interest, would leave me to be the one to deal with them; when she could no longer stomach their wasted affections and advances, she'd dismiss them, coldly.

From the very beginning I knew, Other Self was not benevolent and that I should take caution when leasing my mouth and body to her, but I still did it haphazardly and carelessly. When Other Self began over stepping my hold completely, my mental grip on my self was like my physical grip on the air around me. But still, I was unfazed by this and felt contented with my now co-owned body. After all, I had become what I wanted, I was accepted by those around me, and I wasn't weird to them anymore. My reckless behavior and attitude made me interesting to those who had once cast me aside, and even though it wasn't truly me behind these new behaviors and traits, I was the face they all saw. Other Self wore me like a full body costume, basically, I was the puppet and Other Self was the puppeteer; I was a fool.

Towards the end of my eighth grade year, my father came to see me one day after school, and although I was overjoyed to see him, Other Self, did not share the same elation. The things that were said to him and in the condescending way they were, made me want to cry but with Other Self in control, I was no more than a bystander. Other Self had taken over completely and I was too slow to even realize it. I tried screaming out, I wanted to throw my body to the ground and thrash until the other side of me fled, but nothing happened. Not a sound was made, and not a single action occurred. Unlike me, Other Self, ignored my presence completely. I was now fourteen years old and merely an onlooker in my own life, watching myself do and say things that I did not have the gall to. After what seemed like months of trying to reclaim myself I had given up. Trapped and alone with nothing I could do and nowhere that I could go. In a fit of despair I let sleep consume me.

Ch. 5

In My Absence

For a while, I chose sleep over reality and blissful ignorance over true control over myself, but something awoke me. In my absence, Other Self, had been living life as quite the delinquent. I tried reasoning with her but my words seemed not to reach her. I assumed then, that she could not hear me, so I started criticizing everything she did. But after a few times, Other Self began to heed my advice on a few things and I knew that my assumptions were wrong. If I could not escape my captivity, at least I could bug my captor. My critiques became harsher, my rants grew longer and before long, I knew that Other Self was beginning to get tired of our coexistence. Other Self began doing things; painful things that hurt us both. My body was subjected to constant tattooing sessions, experimental piercings and gaging, my lungs were black from all the smoke I inhaled and my kidneys cringed whenever I swallowed liquid. Despite all these things I remained a virgin. But the rumors about me declared otherwise. I apparently had countless men calling me theirs and even more claiming to have had me on occasion. Other Self was enthralled by all the attention and didn't care if it was good or bad. I felt helpless and ashamed. I was still just the onlooker, a prisoner trapped within the thoughts of a child, governing the stolen body of a young adult. While my consciousness bloomed with maturity, Other Self, still made statements and committed actions like that of a twelve year old. Other Self was egotistical, impatient, arrogant and cunning. Meaning, in the eyes of the world, I was egotistical, impatient, arrogant and cunning. I had become something for my little sister to despise, something for my mother to ignore, and I still wondered if the words to my father continued to plague his thoughts, as they did mine.

When my little sister would try to speak to me I would throw fits so that Other Self would leave her alone. I would yell and scream, beg and plead, with hope that Lil' Bit, would never be influenced by the wolf wearing my skin. Other Self though, found my outcries horridly entertaining and would laugh aloud as she willingly left my younger sister alone. And even though no tears streamed down my face, I felt a sorrow like no other as I watched my little sister grow to loathe me. When my little sister made her last attempt at trying to speak to me, despite my rants and cries, Other Self entertained her question. I tried desperately to reach my still innocent younger sister but the only thing I was hopefully able to convey was a since of warning as Other Self advised her, hoping to set her on a path of no return. In my eyes, it was a path so foreboding even she wasn't prepared to traverse it. I was wrong.

Ch. 6

Childish Ambition

Seeing that she had no 'best friend,' Other Self went to the mall to find one. I tried explaining that finding one was not so simple, but she saw the mall as the place to find whatever you needed. Not knowing exactly how to go about his venture, she chose to randomly walk up to the first lone person she saw and introduce herself. The first person she saw, however was a man who had to be at least thirty, but this did not deter her. She introduced herself, then asked, "wanna be my best friend?"

Which he of course took as an invite to be more than friends, saying, "Sure! So where do you want to go do this?" I explained to Other Self that he expected a sexual favor, rather than the true friendship she sought; she slapped him and began her search again. After wandering the mall for some time, the crowds had begun to dissipate and the stores were becoming empty, but Other Self was determined to get what she wanted. So after seeing a girl around my little sister's age standing alone, she approached her. To my surprise, the girl actually befriended me, I mean, Other Self. I figured that meeting this girl must have been fated, because before I lost control, I never found what I needed or wanted by just waltzing through the mall.

After finding a female best friend, Other Self was determined to attain a male best friend. I told her it wasn't possible, but she went and did it anyway. And even though, I could see that true friendship was the last thing on his mind, Other Self and her new friend, Reece, seemed to ignore his lustful glaze and Cheshire-like smile. But after realizing that Other Self also wanted something more from her male best friend, I knew that it was only a matter of time before Other Self did something she could not undo.

On one warm October morning, Other Self, spoke to me directly. In my own voice she said, "I think it's time we stopped messing around and really got down to business." From my right pants pocket, she pulled out an old condom that had been given to me by my worried middle school counselor, and with my left hand I grabbed a safety pin from atop my dresser. I began to scream and rant but Other Self merely laughed aloud. I watched my thumbs as they texted Kevin, her so called male best friend. It was my thumbs which invited him over, my hand that opened the door to let him in, my feet that lead him to my little sister's room and my lips that told him, 'do it.' And after what seemed like an hour but was more like three minutes, Other Self, had managed to ruin things beyond what either of us could have ever comprehended. I wanted to scream, I wanted to vomit, I wanted to die, I just wanted to forget everything.

Ch. 7

Tormented Mind

I stood naked in the mirror, rubbing oil on my now bulging belly, looking at the stranger I knew to be my own reflection. With tattoos covering most of my body, and gauged holes and piercings everywhere, the only thing that made me recognize myself, as myself, was the absence of anyone else in the room and the way I and my reflection mirrored one another. The tiny life within me kicked, squirmed and jolted, making her presence known. I felt sick knowing I was only a few months away from giving birth to a baby that neither I nor Other Self, truly wanted. And when she was born, nothing changed. Other Self named her, 'Oviaunnce,' the same thing I called one of my dolls from long ago; it was an ugly doll, with creepy eyes, constantly sheading hair and discolored clothing. Regretfully, I could not feel any differently for the baby that came from within me than I did that hideous doll I abused years ago. My little sister hated her just as she did me, especially after Other Self regaled her of the day she was conceived and knowing the story behind the name made her refrain from ever calling her by it. Because of the argument with my mother while I was pregnant, Other Self was working hard to convince Kevin to let her move in with him and his family. Apparently, Kevin's father was a stickler for education and the fact that *I* had dropped out after only a year of high school, made it difficult for him to accept me. I didn't want to leave high school, I enjoyed the people and the popularity, I even enjoyed the work sometimes, but Other Self felt it was wasted, valuable sleeping and TV watching time. Needless to say, I gained quite a bit of weight because of the pregnancy combined with Other Self's laziness. I'm sure, Lil Bit, was disgusted by me, by the way I looked and the person I had become. I hated myself, I pitied myself and I began to reject myself. I wasn't the only one either.

After dad's return home, he stopped talking to me, and Reece stopped coming around. And with my time limit nearly up, I left Oviaunnce in my mother's care, and went to live with Kevin. I still longed to embrace my little sister who had grown dark and jaded in my absence. But with no way to reach out to her, I am forever lost to her. And now, as I begin to forget my own existence, I will once more allow sleep to consume me, and maybe someday the time will come for Other Self to leave and I will be my true self once more.

Part Five

Evanescent Affair

Ch. 1

The Daily Grind

"Who ever heard of a waitress who gives lap dances on the side?" He teased, "I'll throw in somethin' extra… if you can gimme a lil' somethin' extra." He smirked as I twisted in his lap and posed seductively. Each second felt like an hour, but thankfully, it wasn't too long before his desire grew too much for him to handle.

"Nah, I'm good." I said nonchalantly.

"Common Lay-Lay baby," he begged.

I took the sixty dollars from his shirt pocket and tossed him back a five and said, "go home Peter, its closin' time."

And that nasty bastard had the nerve to say, "Sure, I'll just have to see you again tomorrow, then." I didn't even want to see him today. But between the tip from the steak, peas, diet coke and a lap dance I got over eighty dollars from him. As much as I hate what I do, I won't mind seeing him again, or Fred, or Paulo, or any one of those other perverted fools who walk in here claiming they come strictly for the pie, when they all know they come for the cake. I need every penny I can get. My childhood goal was to retire at forty-two and to not be an alcoholic, but something's just gotta give. After a long day of serving assholes, I think I need a drink. I deserve it.

Ch. 2

Humble Beginnings

My life has never been easy by any means. I grew up in a small house in the hood, with two younger brothers, an alcoholic mother and a real Casanova of a father. When I turned fifteen, my youngest brother went to jail. At only thirteen years of age he got thirty-five years to life, not for the robbery, or the fifteen ounces of marijuana on him, or the three guns stashed on his person, but because he ran over a dog during his failed getaway in a stolen police cruiser. When I turned sixteen, my other brother ran away from home, rather than just coming out of the closet. It's not like we all didn't already know which team he was batting for. But sadly to say, it's a decision that got him killed in a state where he couldn't even get a decent burial. When I turned seventeen, not many eventful things happened besides the usual; daddy was sleeping around and momma threatened to shoot him where he stood if she ever caught him with a "heifer," as she liked to call the hoes he constantly flirted with. When I turned eighteen I met a strange boy named David. He walked right up behind me and slapped me on the butt. So I did what any self-respecting girl would do; I threw him on the ground and beat the foo-foo-stoo, outta that boy. What really surprised me though was that only hours and many apologies after that, we were dating. And only a few months after that, my momma shot my daddy in the leg and kicked him out of the house. After I explained to David what had happened, he dredged up the gall to ask me to marry him and before I even realized it, I was pregnant.

The doctor told me I would be having twins, but a few months into my pregnancy, one disappeared and a few months later my first baby was born. I named her Jalisa, after a girl I can barely remember. All I can really say about her is that she was my friend from Sunday school, way back when I was a young girl; misbehaving and still stealing candy from my mother's purse.

Three years later I gave birth to my other daughter. Sadly I don't have a reason for naming her what I did. She's not named after anyone, I just happened to come across the name in a baby name book, and thought it was cute. I don't worry about her as much as I do, Jalisa. Baby J, as I sometimes call her, has always been a bit strange, when she was a baby it was as though she was constantly having a mini power struggle within her own head. Her moods changed constantly and nothing's changed since then. Even now, I feel like I don't know the girl I gave birth to, and maybe I truly don't.

Ch. 3

Promises

Women always know when their man is no longer theirs alone. David first showed that he was interested in someone else one night at dinner while I was still pregnant and having terrible cramps. Jalisa was acting out and as David tried calming her down he looked over at me and asked, "Are you happy?" He didn't say it in a patronizing or aggravated fashion; it seemed like he was crying out in a way, as though he need me to reassure him that our family was a happy one.

I looked him in the eye and said calmly, "happy is as happy does." I regret what I told him next, because I think it gave him the wrong idea. Unthinkingly I said, "If you're not happy, maybe you should go find something that does make you happy." Only a short while after that night, I started over hearing him on the phone whispering about things we never did together. He began leaving the room to text and even started buying me random gifts. There's nothing worse than a gift given out of guilt, and I know they were, because when he'd give them to me he'd say, "you know I love you, right?" Of course I never accused him of anything, I didn't need to; there's something about watching a man lie that I have always found so very entertaining.

On the day my youngest was born, David was nowhere to be found. When you make a promise to someone you love, it means a lot to you; but when you make a promise the tiny person who just came out of you, you do whatever you can to keep that promise. I promised her that from that day on, I'd live for her and Jalisa. I vowed to work hard, to give them a life like I never had, but also, I promised not to shoot they're ignorant ass daddy, as my momma had done mine.

Ch. 4

Hostility, Hostility

After seven years of marriage, I was confronted by a woman who claimed to be my husband's longtime girlfriend. We happened to meet by complete happenstance. I was getting a last minute wedding gift for my boss, from the mall and happened to see David with some chick, I didn't recognize. So I walked over to confront him, but before he saw me headed their way, he rushed off, I assumed to the restroom. So I did what any one would do in that situation; recon.

"Hi," I said to her. "I'm looking for my cousin. I could have sworn I just saw him over here-"

She interrupted, "Oh, is his name David, by chance."

"Yes." I blurted out, giggling awkwardly.

"Oh, yeah, he went to the restroom, he should be on his way back any minute now."

I knew there wasn't much time before he returned so I went ahead and asked, "what is he to you, if you don't mind me asking."

"My boyfriend," she said unashamed, "todays our three year anniversary."

"Oh… that's… nice…" I tried to say it as pleasantly as possible, but I'm sure I sounded just as peeved as I really was. And before I could even put the little hoe in her place, David graced us with his presence.

"Lalaine!?" he cried out, "what are *you* doing here?"

His *girlfriend*, was shocked by how shocked he was, and said stupidly, "you didn't tell your family about *us*?"

It was the perfect set up for me to say, "Damn straight!" He looked mortified and she smiled obliviously.

I had to stop and take a breath before I said something I might have later regretted, and continued in a calmer tone, "David, I think there's a need for introductions, I don't seem to have met your *girlfriend*." I shook my finger at him, "three years… Ha! I bet you thought you were real slick, huh?"

She chimed in again, "David, come on Honey, introduce me."

"Casey, this is Lalaine." He pause and I gave him a look that, had he not already gone to the restroom, would have surly made him piss his pants. He continued the introduction, "Lalaine is my wife… um… Lalaine, this is-" I put my hand up to stop him as Casey started crying.

"You're married!?" she whined, "I thought we were going to start a family together-"

"He has two children, already." I said to her daringly. I directed my attention back to David. "Tell this silly hoe goodbye, and come on, I have some more shopping to do. Waste of my damn time." As I walked away, David followed at a safe distance, leaving his, now, ex-girlfriend standing their crying and alone.

Ch. 5

Winning and Losing

Because I already knew he was cheating, I didn't even hold it against him. I forgave him, not for his sake but for my own, and for the sake of *my* kids. Most people will sin, repent and sin again; its human nature to sin and men are creatures of habit. So when he started cheating again, rather than confront him, I got even. My boss, disheartened to find out that his new wife was less than what he had bargained for, began flirting with me relentlessly. I didn't really mind the extra attention because he was a good looking man and I had planned to quit after the inevitable affair, anyway; Not from guilt or awkwardness but because I hated working in an office answering phones all day. So I figured, 'why not go out with a bang?' Little did I know that *bang*, was going to have a lasting effect.

After being diagnosed with herpes, I of course used it to extort eight hundred thousand dollars from my, then, ex-employer. Seeing no reason to tell my infected husband what I'd done, he went and gave it to whomever he was sleeping around with. It wasn't long after that, that he left; well, to tell the truth, I left him. It's just like a man, to blame a woman for everything wrong with the world. I feel sorry for Eve, whether it was stupidity or gullibility, Adam should have known better. Men never think, 'hmm, what could I have done to change the outcome,' it's always, 'who can I pin the blame on?' Although it was David's cheating that led me to do the same, he blamed me for infecting him, and even had the nerve to demand that I apologize to him and his lil' hoe. I felt bad for arguing with him in front of the girls, but they didn't seem to mind, and I figured, they were better off without him.

As a mother I wanted to show them that they were in good hands. I wanted them to know that independence is a good thing and that men are not the key to success or happiness. To show then that those things are innate, something all people already have within.

Ch. 6

Head of the Household

I made a grave mistake when I chose providing a comfortable lifestyle for my children over actually being at home raising them. Yes, they were clothed and fed. Yes, they never wanted for anything. But I still failed them as a parent. I honestly think that my youngest hates me. Poor Jalisa has just about lost her mind, and all I've really been doing is letting them govern themselves. I was so confident that money was the answer to any problem that might arise that I didn't even notice when Jalisa got some hoodlums name tatted. I had planned to scold her thoroughly, but things came up and by the time I got around to it, she had a second lil' thugs name tatted. And not long after that she was just covered in tattoos. My youngest, though, doesn't seem to be into tattoos and piercings like her older sister. She just mopes around and doesn't do much of anything. I want to be proud of her, but I don't even know what to be proud of. Honestly, I forget about her at times. I don't mean to, but Jalisa just overshadows her by misbehaving, and I think, in a way, she's acting out to get attention. Why else would a nearly grown girl be so very egotistical, impatient, arrogant and cunning. I want to believe that I've just lost touch with how the world works, but I fear I've lost touch with the ones I brought into this corrupt world.

It was only a matter of time before the inevitable happened. For whatever reason, maybe her quiet disposition, I thought it would be my youngest but low and behold Jalisa had become pregnant. "What do you have to say for yourself?" I asked her calmly trying to fathom and truly take in the situation. Primarily the fact that *my* baby, would soon be having her own baby.

I swear I wanted to kill her when those disgusting words left her soured lips. I could have killed my child that day when she sang, "I get it from my momma," she pointed at me and did a little dance as she continued, "like you care." She got teary eyed and asked, "where were *you* when I got pregnant? I did it in your house. But you weren't there to stop me. This isn't my fault... you." She pointed at me accusingly, "you did this to me."

I don't exactly know how it happened but what followed after she said it ended with me holding her by the neck and saying intently, "do you know what I've done-the shit I've put up with to give you a decent life? How dare you blame me for your *mess*." I let her go and told her, "you have two years, to get the hell out of my damn house!" I turned to walk away, but heard her mumble something under her breath. "And that baby may have come out of you, but it's not leaving this house with you. Got that?" She shrugged and that was that.

Ch. 7

Finding Love

At the glamorous age of forty two I retired and only a day after my first grandchild was born. But before I was able to reach my financial goal, I will admit that I did something's most mothers would be appalled by. I didn't have the self-confidence or the downright audacity to become a hooker, but I did become a waitress for a time. And yes, I got some extra cash for providing lap dances to my customers, and I will also admit that I was damn good at it. I was the independent woman I had longed to be. I didn't miss David too much, but I did miss his company from time to time. I never actually dated anyone else. I figured I would die alone, rich and happy, but still, alone. I never imagined that I'd see my estranged husband ever again, but when I saw him, it seemed almost like divine intervention.

"I'll kill'em!" I heard a familiar male voice say, as I put a pack of diapers into my shopping cart. "Who's the father?" The voice was gruff and demanding.

"David?" I gasped. "What are you talking about?!" He circled the cart looking absorbedly at Oviaunnce, resembling a hungry dog rather than to the man I used to love. "Stop it!" I demanded as I stood blocking his gaze.

"Who's that?" He asked still trying to get a good look at her. "Who's baby is that?!" Before I had the chance to yell at him for making a scene, he fell to the floor slowly and cried.

"Get up!" I looked around at the crowd that had formed around us in the small store. Someone who worked there asked me if I needed for them to call security; I declined. "Get up, I'll explain at home."

He looked up at me with tear filled eyes, "can I come?"

I looked at him with contempt and said, "no shit Sherlock."

I explained about Jalisa and her baby, and told him about life for the last few years. He wanted to know mostly about our younger daughter though. I could tell, something had happened between he and Jalisa, but neither of them would tell me what exactly had transpired. We talked, laughed, hugged one another, cried a little and ended up rekindling our love in our daughter's room, on her floor, her desk and her bed. Just as it was fated for me to be reunited with David, it must also have been fate for our youngest daughter to burst in on us.

Ch. 8

Saying Goodbye

David, and I renewed our vows and he came back to live with us. Everything was looking bright and fresh, we were a happy family once more. Granted, it was a very different family though. I was happily taking care of Oviaunnce in place of her deranged mother, David began planning his retirement, Jalisa moved out of the house and my youngest was far away at some college in the middle of nowhere. I wasn't surprised when she announced that she'd be going but I was a bit troubled when she insisted that David and I not come visit her. But things were too good to worry about the small details.

When life is just too perfect, I always seem to wonder, 'what's next.' What will come along and steal my joy, and rip my happiness from my grasp. After three years of blissful, peaceful, undisturbed life, a succubus emerged to take everything away.

I got up to get an after dinner snack while David went to get a glass of iced tea. The doorbell rang and he insisted that he would handle it. I thanked God for him, and his changed ways. But before I could even say, 'Amen,' I heard the most disorienting noise. I ran to the door, and saw him sprawled out on the floor and a young woman standing in the doorway holding a gun.

"Why couldn't you just stay with me…? I loved you…" she said before she raised the gun to her head and took her own life.

I collapsed where I had been standing, to awestricken to move, still in disbelief as to what I'd just been witness to. My mind was in shambles but my body knew that it needed to be by David's side. I crawled to him as I trembled and cried. I tried to call out his name but all I could manage to do was mutter inaudible sounds. I held his limp body in my arms as his blood flowed down his shirt and pooled on the floor, mixing with the blood seeping from his murderer. I sat there covered in blood for hours before the police arrived in response to the gunshots. David was pried from my arms and I was left alone. Only then did I realize the pain I had left Casey feeling, and the pain of the woman who, in turn, took David from me. To make matters worse, my bank account was cleared out by some hacker, leaving me with only the money I was given after the herpes incident. But after paying off the funeral bills and getting new flooring put in where David had died, I had barely enough money left over to pay the bills. But I still felt like Oviaunnce was my second chance to truly do a good job of raising a child. I do not intend to waste the opportunity. But with the lack of funds necessary to be able to spoil her, the least I could do was give her a comfortable life. So I moved into a smaller home, and my days of early retirement were over.

I was unable to get a recommendation for another desk job and thought about becoming a stripper or hooker, but still lacked the self-confidence, so I went back to the diner. And in times like these, every penny counts. It's important to be grateful for another day, even in this unforgiving, uncaring, ambition crushing, mind numbing, wildly corrupt world.

Part Six

Misfortunate

Ch. 1

Fated Day

My cellphone vibrated in my pocket, letting me know that Allen had texted me. As I shuffled through my stash of coins, cash, gum wrappers, keys and what felt like a dead moth, I tried guessing what words of love his most recent text contained. As I pulled my phone out, unlocked it and opened the message, my heart stopped as my eyes scrolled from left to right trying to make sense of what my mind was desperately trying to comprehend. "Thank you for all the love and dedication, I truly think you are a wonderful person and I hope the next guy you meet can see that. You truly are a great girl. Love always, Allen."

"He b-broke up w-with meee..." I bawled, open mouthed and hysterically. I'm sure I resembled a toddler to the countless number of cars and people that passed. I stood there crying until I could cry no more. Although my eyes could not produce anymore tears, my body still shuttered as I breathed and snot continued to drip from my nose despite my efforts to contain it. I was a walking wreck. I tripped, stumbled and even bumped into people a few times, as I walked. I was on my way to pick out an early anniversary gift, but no longer had the need. As I wandered the crowded street I saw a girl about to walk out into the street. I retch out and pulled her back just as a bus passed, honking as it did. The girl jerked free, before turning to face me. I must have looked a mess to her, because my disheveled look made her just stop and stare. I asked her if she was alright, but she looked as though she wanted to ask me the very same thing, but refrained.

She nodded, dusted herself off then said, "Thanks." Modestly she mumbled, "I could have died..." she looked down, "not that I would have minded, but—"

I cut her off, "hey, don't be that way. There's nothing in this world worth giving up your life for." As I tried being strong and reprimanding the girl, I began to cry again. Even though I was telling the girl that life was worth living, I couldn't help feeling like it wasn't. Life without Allen seemed so pointless.

"Hey!" she looked me in my eyes and said sincerely, "I'm sorry for upsetting you."

I chuckled a little and wiped away my tears. "No, it's not you... uhh—"

"Nabara Rosanna," She chimed with a sudden hint of gusto.

"Thank you, Nana." As I said it her expression changed.

"How do you know that name?" her expression seemed very accusing but more embarrassed than hurt.

"I'm sorry, I didn't mean to offend you, it just came to me."

She waved off my apology before saying, "No, no, it's fine. Someone I used to know a long time ago, called me by that name. I guess I'm just not used to anyone else calling me that." She looked down and smiled, "Thanks, for saving me again." She looked up at me awkwardly, "but are you ok?"

I laughed out of embarrassment, "Oh, I'll be fine."

"Are you sure?" She asked politely.

"Yes," I answered reassuringly, "I'm pregnant, that's all."

Her eyes lit up, "Congratulations! Umm... what's your name again?"

"Marie." I told her, now blushing.

We chatted for a few more minutes before parting. As she turned to see if any cars were coming I wanted to tell her to be careful of who she fell in love with but decided not to.

"Watch your step," I called out to her, "carelessness is the express way to deaths door."

Ch. 2

My Life As Marie

Some people would blame others for their downfalls, others blame themselves, while others blame the world or God, and a few blame their fate; I don't blame anyone or anything. I've always been the type of person to take life for what it was, to 'role with the punches,' as my father used to say. But there were times when I couldn't accept things for what they were, times when I had to take matters into my own hands. When I was fifteen I ran away from home. I told my baby sister not to rely on men, but what I really wanted to tell her was, 'don't be like me.' I was leaving home not because I had some horrible life or because I hate my family. I was the average teen back then. Me and my parents argued, I was sent to my room, a few times they tried laying hands on me, and although I defended myself, I never fought back. Me and my parents had a certain respect for one another that made me feel like an adult, and I'm sure it made them feel as though they no longer had control over me. So when I heard them arguing about finances, I decided it was time to leave.

At first I didn't know exactly where I'd go, but after talking it over with Allen, we decided to get a small apartment and move in together. Allen was nineteen, but acted like a thirty year old, I think it was his maturity that attracted me to him, but even before the night I ran away to be with him, I could tell his maturity wasn't as intuitive as mine. On the night I left home, he was supposed to pick me up, but instead I ended up walking over forty blocks to our small apartment only to find him passed out and reeking of booze. I didn't really understand it at the time, but that night should have said it all. I deserved better.

On my seventeenth birthday I woke me up at six in the morning to the smell of bacon, eggs and pancakes, only to find that Allen had made it for himself. When I told him it was my birthday he completely ignored my words and said I should go to the clinic and get checked out. I tried interrogating him as to why I needed a reason to, but he simply shrugged me off and swore nothing was wrong, but he still persisted in telling me to go. Even though my family didn't seem too worried about me having left home, I was still under their medical insurance. I liked to think I was because they secretly cared about me, but I came to realize that they kind of had too; either that or report me missing.

After seeing that the clinic was closed I hopped on the bus, and made my way to the hospital. I sat looking out the window, and heard a commotion at the back of the bus, when an ambulance zoomed past, with sirens blaring. People chatted and speculated, trying to figure out what had happened. I on the other hand, was more concerned with which stop I should get off at.

As I sat in the sterile waiting room I looked over at a girl walking down the hall with a security guard and thought of my younger sister. I wondered how she was, and what she was doing.

"You can't eat that!" I said trying to pull the bar of deodorant away from my infantile sisters iron grip.

"No! I wana!" she protested.

"Stop it, Reece, it'll make you sick!" I yanked the small purple container from her but the actual stick of deodorant was lodged in her tiny mouth. "Spit it out! Now!" She shook her head and slobber ran down her chin. "I'll buy you a push pot if you spit it out." I pleaded. She took a moment to weigh her options before extending her pinky to me. I took her pinky in mines and said, "I promise."

"Miss, the doctor will see you now." The nurse called from the door that I was sitting slightly ajar to. I quickly whipped away my tears then followed her to the examination room.

As I walked through the door to the apartment, Allen shouted, "Happy Birthday!" He presented me with a slice of cake, a small gift bag and a fairly large balloon that read, "Happy Easter."

'He tried,' I said to myself as I opened the gift bag. I pulled out a three pack of Peep's, a pack of skittles and a Visa gift card for twenty-five dollars.

"Thank you," I said before giving him a kiss on the cheek. He smiled, feeling as though he was off the hook. I looked to find the expiration date on the Peep's as Allen coxed me to take another bite of my slightly stale cake. Easter was weeks ago. As I reluctantly ate my cake and Skittles, I thought about my relationship, and finally decided, it was time for a change.

Ch. 3

The Rock, the Hard Place and Me in Between

After putting up with Allen's bullshit for five years, I finally snapped. And when I say, 'I snapped,' I snapped like I had never done before. Although my botched birthday should have been more than enough reason to lash out at him, it was something completely unforeseen. "Get the hell out!" I yelled. I threw anything within arm's reach, I flipped the couch, I yanked the TV from the wall and threw it at the door, I was a tempest with the mouth piece of a sailor. It didn't take much to set me off that day, being on my period and all, I woke up in a volatile mood. But when I came home early from grocery shopping and found him lying in bed having phone sex with some whore, I lost it.

It's strange to think that although he didn't actually cheat, that I know of, the feelings of betrayal was still there. The hurt I felt was still just as agonizing. I needed to clear my mind and so I did something I had only dreamed of. I went to see my family.

After catching two buses and walking just under a mile, I arrived at my old address. I went to knock on the door, but just as I did a woman exited the home. She told me that the old owners had moved, apologizing as she did. I asked her if she knew where they had moved to or any way to contact them. She ran into *her* house, my childhood home, to fetch a small yellow piece of paper; on it was a forwarding address. I pulled out my cell phone to make a memo, but she insisted that I take the paper. The address was written in my mother's very distinct, almost indecipherable cursive handwriting. I thanked the lady then went in search of the house.

As I approached the home, I took a breath as I prepared myself for whatever might happen. But what did happen is something I couldn't have prepared for. A woman emerged from the garage of the home and from a few yards away I said, "I've missed—" Something wasn't right. I stopped my approach as the woman looked me up and down. "You lost?" she asked rudely. A girl emerged from behind her, and gave me the dirtiest of looks.

"No," I said quickly before turning around to leave. I was embarrassed, hurt, abandoned, tired, hungry, all of the above. As I made my way back to the bus stop, I cried.

When I arrived back at the apartment, everything was cleaned up, except for the busted TV, which sat in the corner. If not for that, I would have thought my tirade had never even happened. Allen emerged from the bedroom and as he walked towards me, I lost control over my emotions and cried. He ran the three feet separating us to embrace me before I collapsed. He held me as I cried and I hated myself for it. I wasn't overjoyed or angry about seeing him or the apartment, I wanted to go home, but that option was no longer on the table. As I cried I tried pushing him away but he only held me tighter, making me all the more frustrated. I wanted him gone, and the exact opposite happened, and for a while, I believed it was a good thing. I began to fear losing him and tried my best to keep him happy and within my needy grasp. I didn't know what I'd do if he left, I couldn't handle losing anyone else.

When I arrived at my apartment, it was stripped of everything that belonged to Allen. Not one trace of him was left behind. As I walked through the tiny flat, I began to feel a sharp pain but cast it off as nothing more than cramps; having never been pregnant before, I was completely oblivious to my body's cries of distress. I felt dismayed that Allen had left me, and before I even had time to tell him the news of his child; but him knowing wouldn't have changed anything. I was happy to be having a baby. With no family to return to, I was happy knowing I was about to start my own. But it wasn't meant to be. I awoke, dizzy and disoriented. I put one foot on the floor and one hand on my bedside table, as I tried to emerge from my bed, only to fall feebly to the thinly carpeted floor. I climbed the side of my bed trying to get up, but once I saw my sheets and my blood covered hands I fell to the floor once more. I cried sidesplittingly, screaming and beating my bed in front of me with my fists. I cursed the bed, my nap, myself. I wanted to blame someone or something for my loss, but despairingly, I could not. After calming myself down, cleaning put and washing the sheets, I made myself a nice sized pot of mac and cheese, like my mom used to, and ate it all with tears still streaming down my face. The cheesy noodles seemed to fill my need for sustenance and warmth, but the void left behind could only be filled by a tiny life, and new love.

Ch. 4

Depression and Omission

"Let's go to bed, babe." He kissed my forehead as he took Jordan from my sleepy grip. I lazily got up from the couch and made my way to the bedroom. As I entered the room, Allen had already lain Jordan in his crib, he held out his arms to me, invitingly. I opened my arms to him and we embraced, kissing and hugging, and only moments later I awoke, alone and crying, clinging to my pillow. I was a mental and physical wreck. Having nothing better to do on an early Friday morning I decided to go pick up a latte to cheer myself up.

As I entered the dainty café, a man bumped into me spilling lukewarm iced coffee all over me. I looked down in horror at my white cardigan that was now tinted soggy, hazel brown. I could feel the sweet smelling liquid soaking through to my bra and dripping from my knee length skirt and pooling in my half calf boots. I looked up at him and staring back at me was the most handsome man I'd ever seen in my life. Awestruck, I gaped at him as he pulled out a napkin and held it out to me.

"I'm sorry," as he apologized, his gaze never left mine. I took the napkin but completely forgot why exactly I had taken it in the first place. He extended his hand to me and I shook it. "Hi," he said still gaping, "I'm David."

"Marie," I said, still shaking his hand. We shook hands for a few seconds more before both whisking our hands back at our sides and laughing awkwardly.

"Let me buy you a cup of dcoffee."

"I think I've had all the coffee I need for now," I said looking down again. He became flustered and apologized some more. "It's perfectly fine," I locked eyes with him once more, "it's not every day that such a handsome man spills coffee on me." I laughed timidly, in disbelief of what I'd just said, but he seemed not to mind my forwardness.

"Let me take you out sometime to make up for this," he took out his phone, "will you?"

I gave him my number then answered, "um, I'm free now?"

His eyes lit up and he asked excitedly, "where would you like to go?"

I giggled and picked at my cardigan, "well if you don't mind, I kind of need to change first." He asked me if I need a ride back to my place and I nodded. As we walked back to his car we chatted about this and that, jobs, restaurants, the usual. When we pulled up to my apartment, he offered to stay in his car but I insisted that he come and wait inside. So he followed me up the steps, into my apartment, into my bedroom and before I even realized it, it was six thirty in the evening and we were still lying in my bed butt naked. I had fallen in love once more, but out of shear ignorant bliss, I overlooked something about him that bothered me immensely. He was wearing a wedding ring.

When he was gathering his clothing and other belongings, I asked him about the ring but he simply told me that he and his wife were estranged and that he still wore it to keep his daughters at ease. Once he left, I thought I would never see him again and I began to slump into a brief depression, but only a few days passed before he called me. He asked if I had been to the movies lately, I honestly couldn't remember the last time I'd been, so I told him so and he insisted that we go on a date. It was the first of many dates. And before long he started bringing his eldest daughter along. She reminded me so much of my sister and I tried reaching out to her like a big sister, but she always kept her guard up and wasn't very receptive.

"Reece, come here!"

"No!" tears streamed down my sisters tiny face but she continued to glare at me all the while. "I hate you!" She threw her doll to the floor before screaming, "You're not my sister!"

I reflected on that memory as I looked at a picture of myself, David and little Jalisa. I remembered trying to tell Reece to apologize for breaking my alarm clock, but she refused. I thought of my little sister often, but most of my memories showed just how distant we were. I always wanted a younger sister, and even now I am denied one.

When David came back to the apartment with a bag and a few minor belongings I didn't understand the seriousness of what he had been through. After meeting his *estranged* wife via his cell phone, I was a bit baffled as to where he'd been for the past few days but was more interested in his rattled behavior.

"Listen," he grabbed me by my shoulders and looked me sternly in my eyes before saying, "I need for you to make an appointment." I looked at him questioningly. "Look, I just need to make sure everything is okay, alright?" He smiled caringly, "go see a doctor as soon as you can."

Like an obedient puppy, I obeyed his request and six doctor visits, three shots and two bottles of antibiotics later I was in need of some answers. After his heartfelt confession about sleeping with his wife, who had been cheating on him, I was finally told the truth. He was still seeing his wife, still living under their roof with their two children and I was his side hoe. I was the one he only relied on for sexual satisfaction while his true love and loyalty remained in his wife's diamond incrusted hands. After throwing him out, just as I had done Allen so many years before, I decided to skip the long walk and just take him back. It was as though nothing had happened. It was almost too perfect, I had my apartment, I had my man and all I was missing was a baby. David didn't mind the idea of a baby and jokingly said that he only wanted a boy, so that's what I prayed for. Some prayers are answered without us even knowing and at the unfortunate expense of another.

Ch. 5

Living the Lie pt. 1

After nearly a decade of bliss with my beloved, I finally decided to ask him whether he thought he and I should cement our relationship in the bond of holy matrimony. Meaning, it was time for him to get his divorce finalized. It was something I had allowed him to put off for years, but now, older and wiser, I was ready to be his wife. We had upgraded from my tiny cramped apartment to a slightly bigger, more luxurious two bedroom flat. And even though we both shared to rent and bills equally, it was my name on the lease. Security has always been a vital aspect of everything I've ever had or done. I was suspicious and untrusting by nature and no amount of 'I love you's' could change that.

"Baby sis, you've gotta walk on your own two feet and live by your own accomplishments." I thought of the words I had told my sister as I unzipped my dusty old duffle bag. Still full of tens, twenties, fifties and hundreds, I counted out the seven fifty for rent and bills, then tucked the bag back under my bed. "Don't ever rely on men," I scoffed looking at the money. I told David and anyone else who asked what I did for a living, that I was an 'Off

Cite Distribution's Clerk,' no one ever asked what I did beyond that; Which was a good thing, because I wouldn't know what to tell them. I had made my fortune long ago but still felt the need to work. I refused to go back to my old job though, no amount of money was worth the things I did and put up with. Truthfully, I spent my time writing blogs and starting mess over the internet. Why? Because I simply had nothing better to do. But I longed for something to do, something to make me feel validated in my meager existence. More than anything I wanted a baby, but after several years of trying, I gave up. I was incapable of holding a baby for more than a few months. I slumped into a deep depression and later found that I was unable of even getting pregnant anymore. And because I wasn't technically married, and with a documented source of income, I was unable to adopt, as well. I cursed myself for the life I'd chosen, but fate was still working hard to make things right.

Depressed and lonely after dropping David off at his friend's house for their weekly bout of gambling, smoking, drinking and gossiping, I drove through the dimly lit streets with no real purpose or cause. I saw a girl at a bus stop and thought of all the times I waited alone and in the cold, hoping the bus was the next set of headlights in view. I rolled down my window ready to ask if she wanted a ride, but something about her struck me and I called out to her. As I stared open mouthed at my now grown, baby sister, I waved for her to get into the car. Before she was even fully seated I embraced her and cried. Realizing the neighborhood we were in wasn't the best place for two lone women, I wiped away my tears and drove off. But when she told me what had happened to our mother, and about the woman who had replaced her, I had to stop the car. I thought about the day I had gone in search of my family, and the woman I'd seen. I continued driving as Reece continued filling me in on all that had occurred in my absence. But after hearing that she was pregnant, I was over joyed. And it was obvious that she didn't even want the little bastard. I was finally going to have my dream family. Not wanting to let her and my future baby out of my sight, I insisted that she come live with me. And without even realizing it, I had become obsessed with my dream, my future baby and my future husband.

Ch. 6

Living the Lie pt. 2

Not long after the birth of my sister's baby, I snatched him up, named him and he was mine. No one could tell me otherwise. Even David embarrassed baby Jordan as *our* child. But it seemed as though things didn't work out the way I thought they would. As David's gambling problem grew he began leaving out at random times of the day and night. I could tell that David missed the family that he once had. He would sometimes talk in his sleep, reprimanding or complementing his daughters. I wanted to think it was sweet, but it disgusted me. I was insecure in every sense of the word. I constantly questioned him as to whether he was happy and if he truly loved me. Often times I would just flat out accuse him of cheating, which he of course denied. We argued constantly, but he promised that he'd never leave me and, naïvely, I believed every word. To put my mind at ease, though, I followed him once when he all of a sudden found the need to go the store on lazy Friday afternoon.

To my surprise, he was going to see someone, but it was not another woman as I had suspected. Rather, it was a young woman in the making, his eldest daughter; a girl I hadn't seen in years. I was relieved to see them reconnect at first but after seeing her and hearing the tongue lashing she gave him, my heart sunk and the pleasant memories I had of her melted away. David was practically in tears when he left her there. She was a completely different person, laughing and waving him off. A fire was lit in my eyes and smoke bellowed from my ears. The vanes in my face and fists bulged. Crazy consumed me and before I could even stop myself I was standing directly in front of the girl I used to know as sweet and reserved. She laughed at me awkwardly, as though she was in a state of both distress and bliss. But not having the patience nor the want to find out what exactly had transpired I just slapped her across the face. She laughed then waved me off, just as she had done her father. Every ounce, every fiber of my being told me to beat some sense into that little girl but being the right minded adult that I am, I begrudgingly walked away. But I promised myself that if I ever saw her again, I'd let her have the ass whoopin' she undeniably deserved.

I didn't harass or bug David about where he'd been after seeing his daughter. I pretended not to know, but he admitted everything to me anyway. As I held my man, I knew we were meant to be together and that the incident with his daughter was a blessing in disguise. It was something that pushed him farther from his old family and tightened his bond with me and Jordan. It was clear he wasn't wanted by them, Jordan and I, were his new and improved family. All he, or I, needed was each other.

Ch. 7

The Beginning of the End

On the morning David left, the world was in chaos and I was the only one who seemed to even notice. Everything began to fall apart in the wee hours of the morning, around three. Jordan had awoken in an uproar, with a fever of one-hundred and two point two, he was in desperate need of attention and I was there to nurse him back to health. For times like these, I wished Reece was more helpful, but I reveled in being able to take care of *my baby* twenty-four-seven. After his fever subsided around eight, I went ahead and fixed breakfast which Reece and David scarfed down, fighting over the biggest pieces of bacon and demanding seconds as they vied for more cranberry pancakes, fluffy, scrambled eggs and perfectly whipped Watergate. But still, I was on pins and needles. Deep down, I just knew that something wasn't right. As Reece ran from the house to meet up with some boy she promised wasn't Jordan's actual father, I watched the news as David got dressed to go the store. I began to doze off so David took Jordan from my sleepy grip, and placed him in the bouncer next to the couch, where I was fighting and losing my battle to stay awake. David kissed me on the forehead as he sat my cell phone on small, wooden, coffee table and waved goodbye.

I awoke to the annoying buzz of my cell phone; Jordan was sound asleep and drooling adorably. "Must have forgotten his wallet," I thought aloud as I picked up my phone. But I screamed and threw my phone once I'd read the text, as though it was a cures and the phone was the medium. "No! No! No!" I yelled repeatedly at the phone. My lunatic-like rant was melded with Jordan's screams and whines. Jordan held out his arms to me but I was too busy falling apart to even care. "Not, not, no... he can't... just—" I clawed at my hair in a fit of rage, confusion and grief, "He can't leave!" I yelled, "What about our family!?" As I fell apart, only Jordan was there to bear witness to my tyrannical fit of breaking and smashing everything I could see. I sat in a state of bewilderment, just staring at Jordan. I could see him screaming with tears streaming down his tiny, red face, but heard nothing. But only moments later, when reality set in, did I hear his screams, the smoke detector blaring and my cell phone ringing. But instead of being the doting mother I longed to be, I ignored Jordan. As I made my way from the living room to my room, I grabbed the bleating smoke detector and threw it out of the open balcony window. I figured my phone would eventually die, so I didn't even bother turning it off. I simply went and laid down.

"Marie," Reece stood over me cradling Jordan, "what the hell happened here?" she asked it so intently that I was almost afraid to answer her.

"David left me." I said is plainly without any tears or emotion.

"Well, I think I'm going to hang with my friends later, so I'll help you clean up before I go." Just then she received a call and answered it changing her tone from gloomy and disappointed to happy and bubbly, "Hey Jalisa, what's up."

Immediately, it was as though the room had begun to spin, "who?" I asked trying to right myself.

"Jalisa," she said in a hushed voice, "I'm going to hang out with her and Kevin later." She said it so carelessly, so overwhelmingly nonchalantly that I nearly screamed. But I kept my composure.

'My baby sister had been conspiring against me. She was friends with the enemy all along. I bet she was in on it… the whole thing. She helped take him away from me,' negative thoughts swarmed within my crumbling mind like an angry hive and bee's. I was so caught up in my thoughts that I hadn't even realized when she left. I began to panic. My apartment was clean and there was no sign of her. I began to cry when I heard a faint whimpering sound. There in the bouncer next to the couch was baby Jordan, reaching out for me. I unhooked him, picked him up and then hugged him tightly. "You'll always be mines."

Jordan was all the family I had left. He hadn't left or betrayed me. He didn't leave or disown me. He was my 'one good thing,' and I treasured and spoiled him. I was consumed with waiting on him hand and foot, night and day. I won't admit to missing David, as of this very moment, it's been one year, eleven months and twelve days since he left me. I still have the break-up text saved on my phone. That way I'll always remember his last words to me. But *him*, and those thoughts of false love that lingered haunting me in my dreams, even his smell which I lusted for, it's all just a memory now, the only thing I have to remember him by is a single coat; Which Reece "accidently" wore, stained and bleached. All his other belongings were burned outside in the community parking lot. It was the one time, I actually wished I had a driveway of my own, but nothing would deter me from my mission; purging everything that belonged to, or reminded me of him. They were things I didn't need to hold on to anyway.

Over the past few months, Reece has been becoming more of an annoyance than I can handle. It's bad enough that I'm allowing one of my enemies to live under *my* roof, to eat *my* food, and willingly share *my* personal space. I want to kick her out the day that David left but couldn't bear the thought of her taking my baby with her. So I've been putting up with her trivial whims and wants, I even dropped her off to go conspire with the rest of the enemies a while back. Although, she claimed she was just going to "hang out" with them. But now that she no longer hangs with them, she always wants to take Jordan from me, she even insists on calling him by another name. I fear, one day soon, she will take my child from me.

Ch. 8

Loves True Nature

Having squandered much of my fortune on Jordan, my duffle bag once full of money, was now nearly empty. Amongst the remaining, fives, tens, and twenties, was something I had almost forgotten. I pulled it out, limply, the cold metal weighed more than I remembered but its appearance hadn't changed a bit. I waved it in the air carelessly, but tucked it away when I heard Reece approaching my room.

"Hey," she beckoned from the doorway, "I'm gona go get some ice-cream with Davion, you want me to pick up some for you?"

"who?" I asked in a tone that was more annoyed than confused.

"*My* son," She patted her chest a few times as she spoke, "his name is Davion, not Jordan." She stomped as she retrieved Jordan and as she went to leave she muttered insults under her breath and said, "Don't see why you want my baby so bad, shit, have your own… callin' my damn baby Jordan…"

Fed up with her attitude and her constant interruptions to the life of me and *my* son, I did something I knew I would regret. Just as the front door closed behind her, I opened it and yelled, "Leave and don't come back!" I put my hands on my hips and cursed her out thoughtlessly but after those harsh words left my lips it was as though I had been punched in the gut. I entered my apartment and slammed the front door shut behind myself and fell to my knees, crying. I knew I shouldn't have said all those hurtful things to her, but I didn't know what else to say, I didn't know what else to do. After I calmed myself down, I went and bought a few groceries. I figured Reece would come home eventually. Usually it was her mean words directed at me that would cause us to go head-to-head, then she'd give me a half-assed apologize and everything would go back to normal, but I was the one in the wrong this time. I knew I was the one who needed to apologize and so I figured a nice big dinner, would suffice. I was wrong.

After hours of cooking, a few kitchen mishaps and half a bottle of wine later, there was still no sign of Reece or Jordan. I called her phone several times but got no answer. I decided not to put the food away, thinking she might walk through the door at any moment but she didn't. After that night, I began to lose my mind. The constant worrying and waiting took its toll on me both mentally and physically. Just as I still awaited Reece's arrival, the food did as well. The food on the table hadn't been touched since the day it was made, three months earlier. Needless to say the apartment had a strange, overwhelmingly pungent odor, and tens of flies buzzed incessantly, only briefly halting their annoying activity at night.

As I entered my bedroom, I looked down at my duffle bag which was laid messily beside my bed, just about empty, except for one last remaining twenty dollar bill and the gun that I had never actually used. I sat on the floor almost in a trance and picked up the gun; pointing it at my head and repeating, "pow, pow, pow." I did this for what seemed like hours but as the sun began to set a voice in my head beckoned for my attention.

'Don't blame yourself,' the voice chimed, 'this isn't your fault.

"Then whose fault is it? I did this to myself. I'm all alone and no one cares about me—"

I cried as I tried explaining more of my situation to the voice but it cut me off saying, 'your family deserted you, Allen left you, Reece stole your baby and David...'

My eyes opened wide, "he used me."

The voice then asked me, 'so, what are you gona do? Sit here, cry?"

I nodded.

'No!' the voice exclaimed, 'if you can't have the man you loved, why should anyone?' I picked up the gun and the twenty, stopped off to get a bit of gas, and then headed to David's home. As I sat in my car rethinking my plan to kill the man I loved, something helped me make up my mind. Through the kitchen window, I saw David passionately kiss a woman who I immediately assumed was his wife. I watched as they embraced sensually and rage consumed me. My heart raced as I walked to the front door, rang the doorbell and heard David's steely voice say, "Coming!" I closed my eyes as the door opened in front of me and pulled the trigger.

About the Author

Jackie Navielle was born and raised in Oakland, California. She grew up in a divided home, visiting her father but spending most of her youth under her mothers diligent care. Her development as a artist began when she was in elementary school. Often reprimanded for doodling and daydreaming, Jackie was forced to find a way to cultivate her vibrant imagination and implement it into her studies. She did this by writing and illustrating papers and assignments, sometimes even composing music to accompany them. However, support for her creativity was limited and although her teachers felt she was on the road to success, others wanted her to follow a more clear-cut path. And so Jackie tucked her creativity away, although still doodling and developing her drawing, she chose to write for herself and never allow others to see or judge the stories which flooded her mind. During her Senior year at Santa Fe University of Art and Design, her instructors were introduced to a short story she had written and allowed her to intern under a writer who just so happened to be Mrs. Geraldine Edwards - Hollis. Being such an accomplished and knowledgeable author herself and also the grandmother of Jackie Navielle, their time together and efforts lead to the completion of "The Girl in the Pink Beret Who Sits Alone and Thinks in Silence" the first official book written and illustrated by Jackie Navielle in 2014.